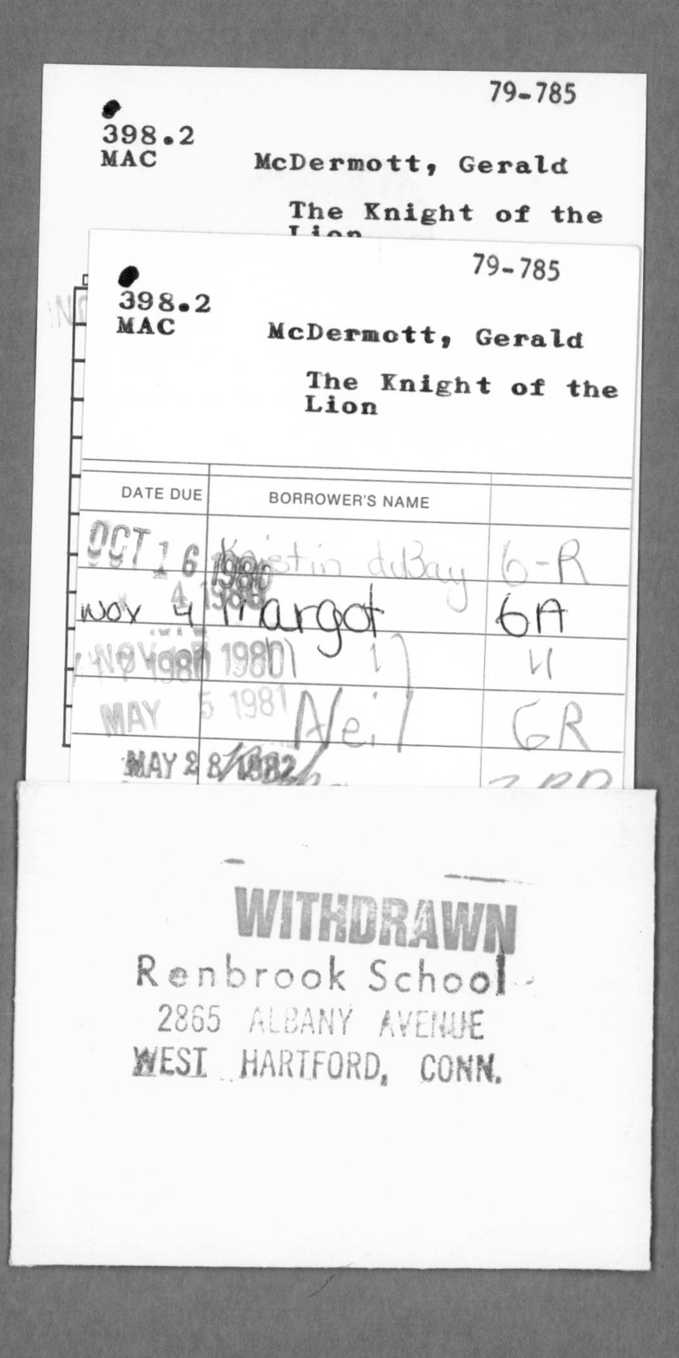
79-785
398.2
MAC
McDermott, Gerald
The Knight of the Lion
79-785
398.2
MAC
McDermott, Gerald
The Knight of the Lion
DATE DUE
BORROWER'S NAME
OCT 16 1980
6-R
Margot
6A
NOV 1980
MAY 5 1981
Neil
6R
MAY 28 1982
WITHDRAWN
Renbrook School
2865 ALBANY AVENUE
WEST HARTFORD, CONN.

THE KNIGHT OF THE LION

THE KNIGHT OF THE LION

written and illustrated by
GERALD McDERMOTT

FOUR WINDS PRESS | NEW YORK

Library of Congress Cataloging in Publication Data

McDermott, Gerald.
The Knight of the Lion.

Summary: A retelling of the adventures of Sir Yvain and his faithful lion, as the young knight goes through several trials to prove himself worthy of a great triumph.
1. Ywain—Romances. [1. Ywain. 2. Arthur, King.
3. Knights and knighthood—Fiction] I. Title.
PZ8.1.M159Kn 1979 [398.2] 78-54680
ISBN 0-590-07504-7

Published by Four Winds Press
A division of Scholastic Magazines, New York, N.Y.

Printed in the United States of America
Library of Congress Card Number: 78-54680
Book design by Jane Byers Bierhorst
1 2 3 4 5 82 81 80 79

THE KNIGHT OF THE LION

I am Yvain,
dark-haired youth of early victory.

I am the fugitive from the Garden of Desire,
I am defiant in the face of Death,
I am the victor and the vanquished.

Twelve hundred leagues have I ridden.
Three black crows,
thirty golden finches,
a lark in a tower,
a nightingale by a fountain,
all have I honored and defended.

I am the Wild Man on the moor,
I am the queller of demons and ogres,
I am the mate of the fiery-maned beast.

I am Yvain,
the Knight of the Lion.
This is my journey
and my story.

I THE QUEST

Night enfolds the granite towers of Arthur's Court. A thousand stars are in the sky, as many as the gems that crown the king's grey head. We love Arthur, the old and gentle sovereign, and gather round him at table to drink ruby wine and feast on roasted meat.

We are strong and noble knights, pledged for all time to our king. As the sun moves steadfastly through the sky each day, so do we move in our knightly round of duty, to honor and defend our fellowship, to perfect our skill at arms, to quest for high adventure. We are the Knights of the Round Table.

Our feast is done and we gather in front of the hearth in the high-timbered hall. We drink again, and tales are told of half-forgotten times. One lame old knight, Calogrenant, stands outlined by the flames. When the others have fallen silent, he speaks:

"My friends, St. John's Day draws near and brings me bitter memory. I have never spoken of this, but tonight, soothed by wine and comradeship, I am moved to tell the tale. When I was young and longed for adventure, I went forth from this castle and plunged into the dark wood. I was in search of a victory that would bring me glory and the awe of other knights.

"I rode for hours through a marvelous forest, thick with trees and blossoms. Toward the close of day, I saw banners fluttering from the towers of a great castle. A Yellow Man reigned there and invited me to rest with him. His castle was filled with the treasures of the world and his fair daughter entertained me. I was tempted to remain.

"On the next day, as I traveled, I met a giant herdsman who rose up before me like a mountain. He was a fearsome creature and wielded a stout iron club. I overcame my terror and asked of him the path to adventure. He pointed the way toward the Fountain of Life which sprang from a miraculous tree at the center of the world. He promised that I should find adventure there.

"And I found adventure. At the center of the world, I came upon a golden chalice chained to a miraculous tree. The chalice rested on an emerald slab close by the Fountain of Life. I dipped the cup into the crystal spring and spilled the precious waters on the dark green stone. At once, a terrible storm broke all about me, destroying every living thing and laying waste the land. A Black Knight came charging forth to defend the Fountain. He rebuked me for misusing its life-giving waters, for bringing death and destruction to his domain. Then he cried out a challenge and thundered down upon me.

"We fought until my sword was shattered and I was hurled to the ground. Lame and horseless, my weapon lost, I painfully made my way back to this court. Though I have faithfully served my king these many years, not a day has passed when I have not been filled with shame at the thought of my disgrace. I have had many victories, but that defeat still haunts me."

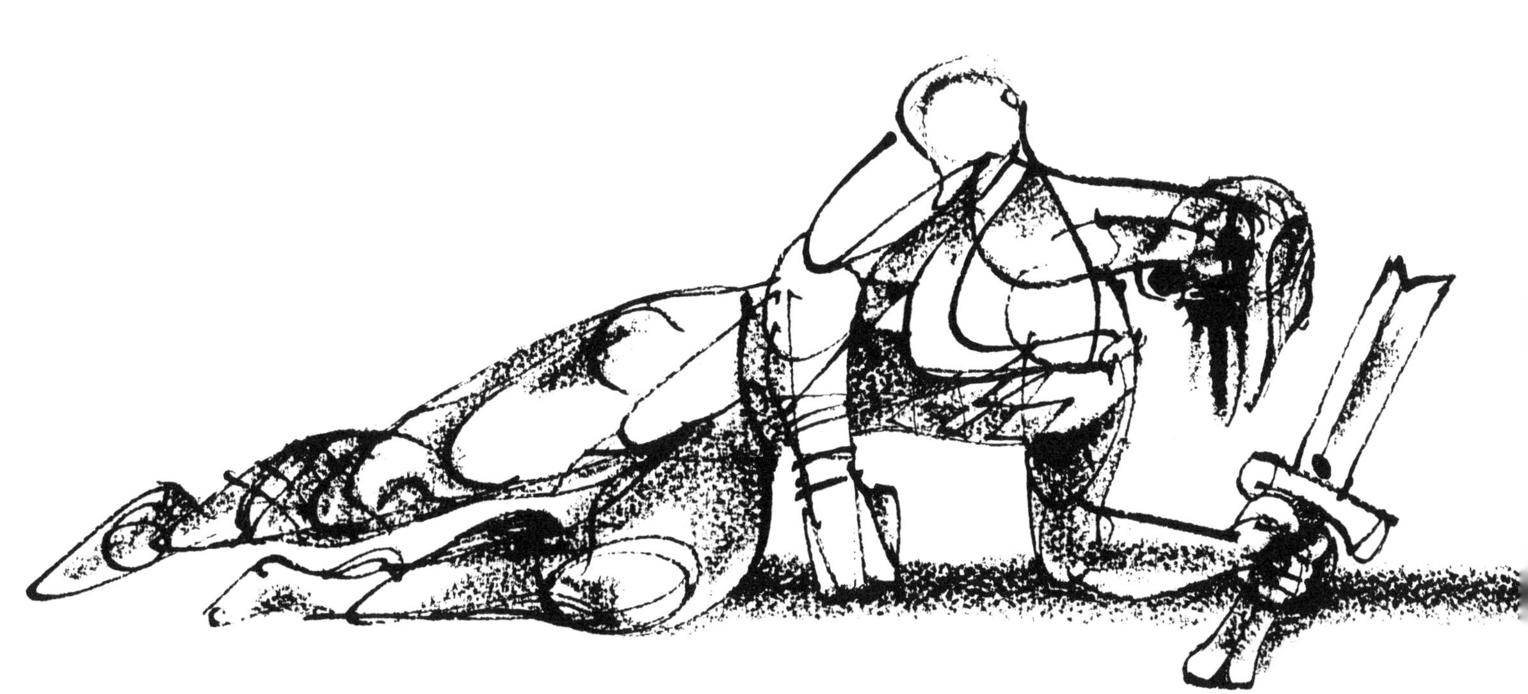

"Nonsense," roars Arthur, and rises up to console his friend. "There is no shame, my faithful knight, for one who has so bravely sought a challenge." Arthur speaks to all. "It is time that we redeem the good name of Sir Calogrenant. This is a marvelous adventure which we will all undertake. Knights of the Round Table, a fortnight shall not pass before we ride forth together to challenge the Black Knight. We shall dash the waters of the Fountain in the face of that rude and unpleasant fellow!"

My companions of the hearth cry out bravely. All assembled raise their wine cups and brandish their swords. They grasp each other firmly and swear upon three oaths that before St. John's Day, they will join Arthur on this quest.

I stand apart in the flickering light of the leaping flames. The sparks of my imagination are kindled and the fire of adventure fills my head. This quest will be mine alone. I will set out before all the others. The glory of overthrowing the powerful Black Knight will belong to me. All will wonder at Yvain, dark-haired youth of early victory.

I saddle my horse in the shadowless light of early morning. I lead him past sleeping guards and through the gates of Arthur's castle. Free of the enclosing walls, I leap upon my mount and gallop toward the beckoning dark forest.

All day I ride through brambles and bushy oak. There is bird-song, the gentle rustle of leaves, and the smell of thornberry crushed underfoot. I trot past unfurling ferns, lichen-covered rocks, circles of mushrooms in the cool earth.

My steed's hooves sink into the soft green moss. Thin fingers of sun reach through the canopy of leaves to touch flower bells. The bark of thick-trunked ancient trees, mottled in green and grey and tan, resembles maps of unknown lands.

I pass through furry blue-green thickets and ford a wandering stream. I smell the musty odor of damp earth and the sap released from broken twigs. There is no path, only a veil of mist. My horse and I are wanderers, we are searchers in the dark wood, always making our way, crushing the lilies and the ferns.

An open vale, a pile of grey-green rocks, a circle of sunlight filled with pale yellow flowers. Who lives here? Unblinking eyes watch us. Unseen noses sniff at our passing.

The end of day approaches and the forest is damp and cold. Spears of orange flash above the treetops. It is the setting sun, caught in the shimmering folds of great silken banners. I emerge from the forest and see a golden castle, the banners flying from its towers. As I approach, the air shudders with the deep reverberation of a hugh copper gong. The gong hangs over the portals of the castle, and beneath it stands the Yellow Man. He strikes the copper once again and yet once more.

"I greet you, Sir Yvain," he calls out cheerfully. This golden-bearded, yellow-robed fellow wears little shoes cobbled from diamond shapes of colored leather. With his bright robes and golden rings, he is radiant and aglow. I begin to sweat and feel weak.

"You appear tired from your long journey. Rest here awhile, my friend," he says, and bows—but not too low, for he is very fat. "I am the Hospitable Host and I have been expecting you. You have come to the Castle of Abundance and are most welcome." He points toward the open gates of his castle.

"Thank you, Sir, but I shall not stay long, for I am in search of the Fountain of Life."

"Ah, we shall see. Tarry with me and with my daughter. The pleasures of my castle are sweeter than the perils of the Fountain." He beckons once more. Tired from my journey, I am anxious to rest. I bless and thank this jolly host, slip down from my mount, and walk through the brazen gates.

All the treasures of the world, it seems, are gathered here in the Castle of Abundance. Mirrored galleries, shimmering with reflections, chambers of gold, chambers of rubies, chambers of light. Alabaster goblets, bowls of Abyssinian fruit, the scent of ambergris. Thrones of precious wood to sit upon, finely woven cloth to lie upon. A golden wine bowl that never empties, a golden plate ever filled with delicious meats.

At night, in the tower garden, the daughter of the Yellow Man yearns to delight me. She caresses me and kisses my mouth. She holds me close and begs that I remain with her in the Castle of Abundance. "Whatever you desire, Yvain, will be found within these walls," she promises.

"What I seek lies far beyond these walls, fair lady. I am in search of the Fountain of Life and will not remain here. Thank you all the same... and good morning to you." I gallop away in the rose dawn. The perfume of the garden still clings to my cloak. As the morning star fades, I ride toward the horizon.

The cool morning wanes. The sun rises high over the plain and I am blinded by the summer heat. My horse falters. We halt.

In a field before us, huge black bulls rage in battle. On a hill, standing herd over them, is a dark and terrifying figure with one eye. The heat of his hairy body makes me gasp. Cloaked in hides, smelling of sweet animal sweat, clutching an iron club in his knobby fingers, One-Eye glares down at me.

"Who might you be?" growls One-Eye.

"I am a knight of good King Arthur's court. And who might you be?"

"I am who I am," grumbles One-Eye. He raises his club and cracks the wind. At the sound, all the wild bulls cry in terror. They leap up in fear and obedience until they are as numerous as stars in the sky.

"I am the Woodward of the Wood!" proclaims One-Eye, "and I have dominion over every creature. All beasts obey me. Little man, will you dare to pass me by?"

"Of course I will, for I am in search of adventure. I seek the Fountain of Life, and *you* are standing in my way!"

One-Eye spits, and laughs, and raises his club again. "Since I do not frighten you, I shall point the way to your adventure. Follow this path and journey beyond the mountain. It is there, at the center of the world, under the branches of a miraculous tree, that you shall find the Fountain of Life. Though the fellow you will meet there may be less agreeable than the fellow you've met here, Yvain . . . Sir."

II THE FOUNTAIN

Stumbling over hot stones, sliding on the graveled path, I ride up the face of the mountain. I ride in the shadows of the granite cliffs. I ride above the nests of hawks and eagles. I reach the summit and look down into a wondrous valley. Scarlet poppies and tangled green vines, purple blossoms and yellow reeds grow there; a rich and fertile land.

Across the valley I see the miraculous tree, its broad limbs spreading wide at the center of the world. Chained to a thick limb is a golden chalice. The chalice rests upon an altar of emerald.

I rush to the tree and seize the chalice. I dip the goblet into the boiling spring. As the vanquished knight, Sir Calogrenant, had done years before, I pour the water upon the dark green stone.

The water strikes the stone. Lightning bursts in my face and throws me to the ground. The sky turns black and boils with clouds. Grey rain sweeps down and sheets of hail tear at me. I lift my shield and cloak against the cutting ice.

Then the wind dies and the clouds roll away, shredded on sharp mountaintops. Silence. I drop my cloak and look about. The land is laid waste. There is no life. There is only dry, cracked earth and the brittle limbs of withered trees. It is a desert that reaches to the horizon.

A sweet song then comes to my ears. Flocks of rainbow-colored birds swarm above my head and come to rest on the barren branches. Where once leaves flourished, now sings a plumed chorus: a melodious foliage.

A crack of thunder silences their birdsong. Rolling thunder shakes the ground beneath my feet. My horse screams in terror. A sudden heat at my back, so intense it burns, forces me to turn. I see a rider garbed in midnight black. He curses as he charges down upon me.

"Intruder! Recklessly have you spilled the waters of the Fountain of Life. You have ruined my lands. You have laid waste this fertile valley. Where there was life you have left only dust and broken stones. Defend yourself, Yvain. Now you will replenish this dry earth with your own red blood!"

Our horses beat across the burnt ground. We crash together. We curse and groan and wield our weapons. The Black Knight's death axe cuts the air beside my head. We turn our mounts and clash and reel back again. I dig my spurs into my steed and plunge forward. I come too near. His heavy axe is above me, poised for a death blow.

I thrust and plunge my sword into his helmet. The dark warrior screams in pain. Thick clots of blood spill from his visor. He clutches his reins and turns to race away.

I pound toward the high ground in pursuit of the Black Knight. A dark castle is on the horizon and toward it the wounded warrior flees. I spur my steed and gain on him.

The Black Knight gallops across the drawbridge and through the open portals. A leap behind, I pursue him. As I rush forward, chains rattle. An iron-toothed gate falls and splits my saddle behind me. Its dagger spikes tear my horse apart and pin his hindquarters to the oaken bridge. With the gate slammed shut behind me and a severed horse beneath me, I tumble forward into the darkness of the castle.

I lie upon hard stones, dark with horse's blood. I am sealed within the stronghold of the Black Knight. Angry shouts echo in the stone corridors. Men, armed with swords and thick clubs hunt the granite hallways. They seek the one who has wounded their lord. Their voices come closer, crying for vengeance.

I hear shuffling behind me in the blackness and then a whispered voice: "Yvain!" I turn to see a young girl emerge from a low doorway. She comes to where I have fallen. "Lunete is my name, handmaiden to the Lady of the Fountain." She looks down at me in astonishment. "Tall and proud young knight, you are smeared with blood and crouch like a hunted animal. You are the one who has wounded my mistress's husband! Now you are trapped and his henchmen are coming near. Quickly, give me your hand."

She presses a jeweled ring into my palm. "Wear this and it will protect you as you walk about the castle. Have faith in me, Yvain, and I shall intercede for you." Quickly she is gone, disappearing in the shadows of the low door. I slip the ring upon my finger and become invisible. Unseen, I wander through the labyrinth of the coal-black castle.

The angry shouts become low moans. Weeping and lamentation fill the air. I stand invisible amidst smoke of incense and burning tapers as a procession passes. The immense corpse of the Black Knight is borne into the hall by shrouded figures and laid upon a marble slab. His deep wound is wine red and his lips are blue with death.

A woman, honey-streaked hair flowing down over her face, comes to the bier of the Black Knight. She shudders with pain and anger, her eyes are swollen and dark with tears. I come silently near. Though her face is filled with pain, it does not obscure the elegance of her features. This is surely the Lady of the Fountain. I wonder at her beauty and at her grief. Why shed choking tears for such a brute?

I draw closer still and stand next to the bier of the slain knight. In my invisible presence, crimson rivulets of blood spring from his corpse. Abruptly, the crying and sobbing of the assembly ceases.

"The murderer is within these walls!" shouts a guard. Swords are drawn. The armed assembly surges out of the hall and scuttles into the dark stone passageways, swearing revenge upon the slayer of their lord.

Now the hall is empty, save for Lunete and the Lady of the Fountain. Lunete goes to her lady's side. With gentleness and respect she seeks to comfort her. "My lady, I know your grief is great . . ."

"I weep not for him, but for my realm. It now lies unprotected. Word has come to me that Arthur and his retinue journey here. They will spill the waters of the Fountain of Life, raise the storm, and await the challenge. Curse those who meddle with the life-giving waters! Though my husband is dead, my land must remain forever living. I must have a champion to defend the Fountain."

Lunete whispers, "I know of such a man, if you will accept him."

"Now that my husband is lost to the world, I doubt such a man can be found," she answers.

"My lady, such a man is in this hall," says Lunete. "Yvain, come forth!"

I draw the Ring of Invisibility from my finger. The Lady of the Fountain is astonished at my sudden presence. She is suspicious and resentful, then enraged. "*You* are my husband's slayer! Do you presume to take his place?"

"I love you, beautiful and gracious lady," I respond and step forward. "I ask that you accept me as your champion. I swear to you my fidelity and courage. I will do anything that you desire."

The Lady of the Fountain fixes the gaze of her golden eyes upon me. Then, without speaking, she turns and leaves the hall. As Lunete dutifully follows, she calls back softly: "I think she likes you not a little."

Amid song of bells, merry shouts and laughter, I am wed to Laudine, the Lady of the Fountain. We are encircled by bright faces, dancers whirling, ribbons streaming. We are showered in cascades of flower-petals. Children stand on tip-toe to watch the happy procession.

Our wedding feast lasts seven days and seven nights. Each day is increasingly joyous. Each meal is more sumptuous than the one that precedes it: more meat, more fruit, wineskins bursting. Sun fills the courtyard where we sing and dance in celebration.

Crack of thunder. The sun is masked and clouds roll across the sky. Our table is hushed as the storm wind howls, the sky grows grey, then turns black as pitch. There are distant hoofbeats. The earth quakes.

All look to me. My lady speaks, "Yvain, now you are the defender of the Fountain."

Slowly, I rise. Guards surround me and buckle me in black iron. They cloak me in black velvet. The heavy helmet is forced down around my head and covers my face. My breath is trapped within the iron casing and I sweat beneath the weight. Lifted up onto a black and armored charger, I pound out of the castle, across the land stripped bare, toward the Fountain of Life.

Under the bird-filled branches of the miraculous tree, King Arthur and his Knights await. I charge down upon them, masked and unrecognizable to my old comrades. I bellow forth the challenge, as best I can.

"You have violated these... my lands and now must defend yourselves for spilling the Waters of Life!"

Arthur smiles and signals his knights to attack. One after the other, they rush forward, waving sword and brandishing mace. One after the other, I unseat them and send them sprawling to the ground. Arthur, stunned and ashen-faced at my facility, sends forth his remaining knight. My opponent lunges and turns most skillfully. He is good but I am better. I catch his buckler with my lance-point and send him somersaulting into the mud.

A scattered crew of unhorsed and shame-faced knights, an open-mouthed Arthur, all watch intently as I lift up my visor. In a chorus of recognition, they cry, "Yvain!"

"We feared you had perished at the hands of the Black Knight," says Arthur with relief.

All gather round and I tell of my adventure and victory. Then I invite my old hearth-mates to the final day of my wedding feast. I lead the noble, motley crew laughing and stumbling up the hill.

Arthur bows before Laudine. She graciously welcomes the king and his knights into the precincts of her castle.

Our wedding feast ends. King Arthur and his men prepare to leave. Arthur comes to me and pleads, "Yvain, why not return with us? We have missed your presence at our court. Honor us with a brief visit."

I turn to Laudine and look into her golden eyes. "Let us join my friends at Arthur's court."

"I shall not go with you, Yvain. If it pleases you to go, then do so. Take this emerald ring to remember me, and promise to stay no longer than a year from this day—St. John's Day."

"Yes, of course, though I will probably return much sooner," I reply.

"If you fail me, Yvain, if you do not return one year from this day, my love will turn to hate."

Yellow and blue, gold and orange, our banners unfurl. Hands are raised in salute, proud-necked horses jostle and clatter through the portals of the castle. We depart, Arthur, his loyal knights, and I. At the bottom of the hill, I turn to wave farewell to Laudine. The gates of the castle are already closed.

I languish in the golden autumn days at Arthur's court. With good friends, I laugh and joust and feast. The Fountain seems an eternity away, yet I shall soon return. I shall return before the snow begins to fall.

Then winter trims the castle in white fur, white crystals fall from the sky, geese call, ponds are glazed hard. The world is cold and too bitter for travel. While the winds howl, we noble knights gather in rush-strewn halls. In front of the hearth, we grow drowsy over wine and endless games of chess. I shall return to Laudine when winter dies.

Raw spring and hearty shoots, green as the emerald of my ring, emerge between shrinking crusts of muddy ice. The sun reigns once again. The grain is in the furrows. Sweet air draws us forth from hibernation. I would depart from Arthur's Court, but the roads are muddy and impassable. In time, I shall return to Laudine.

Summer comes, the air is hot and hazy yellow. I lean against the jousting post, at ease in the warm sunlight. Nearby, my fellow knights cavort and joke as they prepare a merry tournament to mark St. John's Day.

My heart shakes. I clutch the emerald ring upon my finger. St. John's Day and a year has passed since I left the Lady of the Fountain. I cry out as one waking from a dream.

A rider appears at the crest of the hill. It is Lunete. She crosses the meadow and reins to a halt in front of Arthur's Castle.

"Yvain," she says sternly, "you are a liar and a hypocrite. You are a faithless coward and a thief of the heart." I look at her but cannot speak. My tongue is dead. Hot tears scald my eyes and run down my face.

"Yvain, you have abused my lady's faith and trust. You have forgotten your pledge. You have left her unprotected and for this she rebukes you."

Lunete leans from her saddle and seizes the emerald ring from my finger. "A man deserves this ring, not a boy!" She turns and gallops through the meadow, over the hill, and into the darkness of the tangled forest.

I stumble forward as she rides away. "Wait! Wait! I am a fool! Forgive me!" Tearing at my hair, ripping my shirt, I push aside those who rush to stop me. Screaming and running blindly in the thickets, I trip over dead branches. Friends pursue and then lose sight of me. I am running in the swampy forest. I am running, crying, falling. Branches clutch at me, briars tear me. Bleeding and drooling, I crawl through the dead leaves. I chew on roots, I vomit in streams. It is dark and wet and I am cold. All is lost.

III THE RETURN

An old Hermit, with gnarled hands and leathern skin, finds me alone in the deepest part of the forest. "Here is food," he says. The Hermit offers moldy crusts of bread and urges me to eat. "You have been mad and like a beast run naked in the forest. Your soul is sick and your body is dying. Now eat of this and it will sustain you, for your journey is about to begin.

"No, no!" I cry. "My journey is at an end. All is lost. I have squandered my perfect life, my beautiful kingdom, my honor, my Fountain, my love. All is lost and I am dead."

"You cannot lose what you have never won," replies the Hermit. He retreats into the shadows of his cave and says, "Go forth, Yvain. Three black crows, thirty golden finches, a lark in a tower, a nightingale by a fountain: all await you. You must honor these winged creatures before your own spirit can take flight. These will be the blood-red days of your journey." The Hermit vanishes into the darkness of the cave.

"Wait!" I call out to him. "How am I to do these things? How shall I return to the Fountain?" The Hermit chants a mysterious song:

> Ride on, ride on,
> Yvain, my son,
> twelve hundred leagues on horse of dun,
> 'til foes are slain and honor's won,
> 'til moon is swallowed by the sun,
> 'til circle's closed and journey's done.

"You mock me!" I shout. "I have no steed to carry me twelve hundred leagues. I have no weapons. I am weak and exhausted. My body is covered with sores. Yet, you mock me." I weep until my eyes are sealed with sleep.

I awake to see the sweet white faces of three women cloaked all in black. I lie in the marble hall where they have brought my broken body. They salve my wounds with magic herbs.

"Yvain, you are healed." They garb me, give me armor and weapons, and a dun-colored horse. I lead the horse to a pool, so that he may drink. Kneeling down, I see my own scarred face reflected in the water. My eyes are dark with shadows, but a fire dimly flickers there.

I thank the crow-cloaked women. "You have restored me and I will not forget your compassion. Now I may begin once again. Now I may return to the Fountain." I mount my horse and say farewell. We leap over the low stone wall and begin our journey.

Ride on, ride on,
my horse of dun,
twelve hundred leagues are to be run,
'til foes are slain and honor's won,
'til moon is swallowed by the sun,
'til circle's closed and journey's done.

At length I pass into a rocky landscape. In the distance, I hear strange and terrible cries. Searching out the sound, I see a black dragon of scaly hide coiling about a cleft in the rocks. Trapped in the cleft, a snarling ruddy-maned lion evades the dragon's poison tongue.

"O king of beasts, I cannot pass and leave you in this plight." Without another thought, I lunge forward, thrust out my lance, and kill the hideous serpent.

The lion emerges from the rocks and bows before me. Tears are in his eyes as he looks to me with thankfulness. I smile at the grateful beast and turn and ride away.

I have ridden quite far when I am amazed to see the lion loping just behind me. I pull up my reins and call to him. "It's thanks enough you've given me, brave monarch of the animals. Now, please go home young lion. I must ride on." But still he keeps apace, over rocky paths, through pine forests, and swampy marsh. I stop again and plead with him. "Go home, I say, for I've a long journey that will only end when I reach the Fountain of Life. Go home!" No use, the lion stays with me as I ride.

At day's end he brings me meat. We eat together at the fire: strange dinner companions. The beast is happy and stands guard over me as I sleep that night.

We set forth in the morning mist, my lion-mate and I, for I am eager to find the Fountain and return to my dear Laudine. We have not traveled far when I see the long sleeves of a young girl's robe fluttering from a tower. As we draw near, the maiden cries out to me. "My lord, you must help. I've been unjustly imprisoned here."

I realize at once this is Lunete, who befriended me within the walls of the Black Castle. I am helmeted and cannot be recognized. I do not speak my name. Instead, I call up to her and ask why she has been thus imprisoned. "A wicked seneschal has falsely accused me of betraying my Lady. I encouraged her to marry Yvain, who proved to be a faithless coward and left her undefended. For my error, the seneschal and his sons will come here in the morning to punish me. They will burn me alive!"

I am heartsick that I have been the cause of Lunete's imprisonment. I am desperate that she might die because of my failings. But I cannot release her from this tower without the seneschal's key. I pledge on my life that I will return in the morning, to defend and deliver her from her captors. My lion and I then seek shelter for the night.

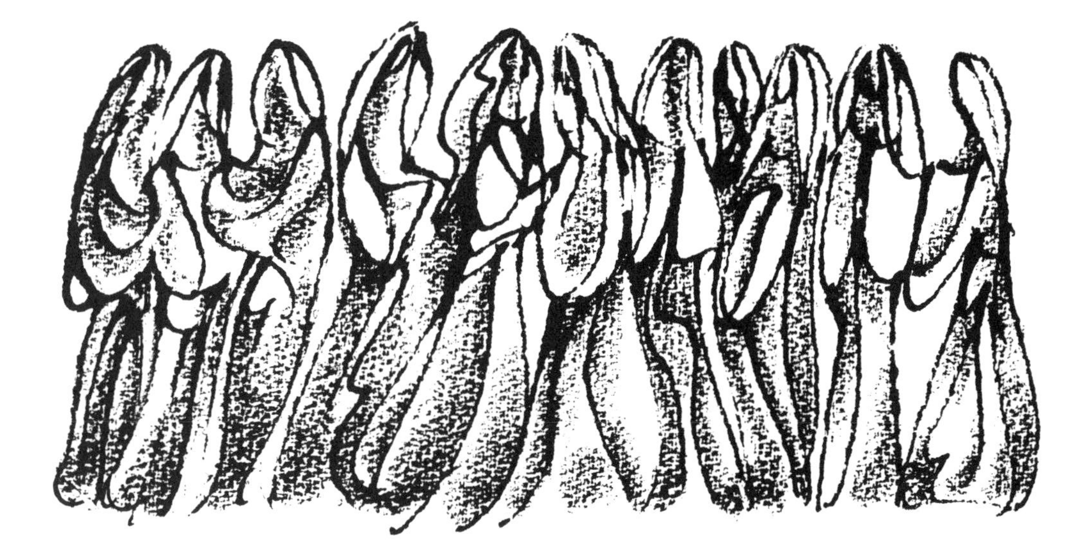

The sky is dark when we finally come to rest. The lion and I are welcomed by the goat-bearded lord of a crumbling manor. We are grateful that he gives us supper, but as our host serves us his hands tremble.

"Does my lion frighten you, my lord? Do not be afraid. He is really very gentle in the presence of friends."

"No, no, good sir, it is the Harpin of the Mountain who terrifies me! I am unable to pay him tribute and tomorrow morning he will come to slay my golden-haired daughters—all thirty of my beloved children." Upon saying this, he begins to weep, then pleads with me. "Brave knight, will you champion them and save their tender lives?"

I am moved by his plea, but think first of my promise to Lunete. "My lord, I cannot refuse you, but I must finish the fight by early morn. I am pledged to another combat tomorrow and must not be delayed."

He thanks me and weeps even more. This night I sleep uneasily.

The day begins and we await the Harpin of the Mountain. I think of Lunete, trapped in her tower. I must not break my pledge to her. Each moment that passes brings Lunete closer to the flames. Where is this ogre? I hesitate, and pace back and forth, my lion pacing with me. Desperate with indecision, I begin to saddle my horse as the sun climbs in the sky. Then the thud of heavy footfalls echo through the valley.

"I am the Harpin of the Mountain and I have come to collect my tribute," the ogre roars.

"The only tribute you'll have is the point of my sword," I shout in response. "I am Yvain, champion of these thirty golden maidens, and no harm shall come to them. I challenge you!"

The Harpin looks at me and at my bristling lion. "With a wild animal at your side, yours is a weakling's challenge!"

"That cannot be denied." And so I lead the lion behind the wall and shut him in with chain and iron gate. He begins to cry and scratch. He paws at the iron bars. "Now stay there, loyal friend, for this fight shall soon be finished."

I turn to face the Harpin and as I do his gristly fist strikes me full force in the mouth. My teeth shake and I fall backward to the ground. The lion cries as though wounded and leaps at the door of his enclosure. Dazed, I wipe my bloodied mouth.

The lion roars and leaps over the confining gate. His ivory fangs sink deep into the Harpin's arm. I regain my feet and now we both attack the Harpin, striking and tearing until he collapses headlong under the force of our dual strength.

The lord, his daughters now spared, rushes to thank me and bind my wounds. Though I am bruised and bleeding from the Harpin's blows, there is no time to be soothed by my grateful host. Death draws near for Lunete and I am pledged to rescue her.

My lion-mate and I gallop toward her tower.

Ride on, ride on, fleet-footed dun,
faster, my fiery-maned one,
six hundred leagues yet to be run,
'til foes are slain and honor's won,
'til moon is swallowed by the sun,
'til circle's closed and journey's done.

We return to the tower and see the wicked seneschal and his sons piling brush and twigs high around its base. Already the three brutes hold lighted torches, ready to touch them to the pyre. Lunete is to be consumed by the flames.

We charge down upon the churls with a fury. They turn and thrust their searing brands in the face of my lion-mate. He howls in pain. Enraged, I descend upon them with sword and shield. First one, then two, then three fall down, twisting and disgorging blood, aflame with the fire of their own torches, screaming and writhing in miserable death.

I take the key from the seneschal's belt and release Lunete from the tower. Then I gently lift the limp form of my faithful lion friend, weak from his burns and wounds. I lay him lengthwise on my shield and place him across my saddle bow.

"Thus shall I carry you, my lion-mate, until you are healed."

We ride slowly toward the forest. Lunete, now free, calls out in gratitude. "Brave knight, who shall I say has delivered me from the fire? To whom should I and my mistress be grateful? What is your name?"

"The Knight of the Lion," I respond softly. Then I turn and ride slowly down the bramble path, carrying my wounded friend.

In time, with love and magic herbs, my faithful lion is healed. I resume my urgent return to the Fountain and to my dear Laudine. We race through a bleak winter landscape, where grey melting snow reveals hidden sprouts of green. We race over frozen rivers that crack and groan under our weight. We race over the frosty bracken. Cold and damp precede us, ice and bitter wind follow us as I sing:

Ride on, ride on, my hearty dun,
no rest for us, my faithful one,
three hundred leagues yet to be run,
'til foes are slain and honor's won,
'til moon is swallowed by the sun,
'til circle's closed and journey's done.

Trotting downward into the fertile valley, the lion close at my side, brushing past the fragrant blossoms and tangled vines, we follow the familiar path. One league to run and we reach the emerald altar in the shade of the miraculous tree. Once again, I lift the golden chalice and plunge it into the seething waters of the Fountain of Life. Once again, the droplets hiss like steam as I pour the crystal liquid on the dark green slab. Once again, the storm sweeps over us. Masked and armored, I stand beneath the barren tree and wait.

Silence. Far off, I can see the cracked walls of the Black Castle. The gates groan open, but there is no pounding thunder. No black-cloaked rider charges forth from the portals to defend the Fountain. Instead, there emerges the slender figure of Laudine. She is followed closely by Lunete. Slowly, reluctantly, they approach the Fountain.

Laudine speaks. “Sir, we have no defense. My youthful husband has long fled, unworthy, and now my kingdom is at your mercy.”

“I do not come to harm you,” I say. “I come to protect and be faithful to you.”

“Shall I believe you? What gives you the right to be my champion?”

“I am the Knight of the Lion. I have been blessed by three black crows, I have defended thirty golden finches, and I have released the lark from the tower. Now I come to honor the regal nightingale.”

The Lady of the Fountain turns to her handmaiden. “Lunete, can you make sense of this fellow’s riddles? He is either a poet or a madman.”

“My lady,” Lunete answers respectfully, “is he not the same brave and gentle knight who released me from the tower, who delivered me from death by fire? Perhaps he has come not to enslave us but to serve us.”

“Perhaps.” Laudine looks at me and at my lion-mate with suspicious golden eyes. “If you are ready to serve me, I will accept you. Let me first see your face.”

I remove my helmet. Though my cheeks are scarred and a beard grows where once had been the smooth face of youth, Laudine recognizes me.

"Yvain! You have tricked me."

"Lady of the Fountain, the man who kneels before you is not the boy who failed you. Entranced by colorful flags and knightly jousts, I wandered from your side and lost what I had so easily won. Endless leagues have I traveled, painful wounds have I endured to come once more to you. Now, just as my lion-mate has defended and served me faithfully, so shall I honor you. I love you, Laudine, and pledge myself to you."

Laudine peers into my eyes. She steps toward me, pauses, then touches my face with her slender hands. She leans forward and kisses my brow. I rise and hold her tenderly. We embrace as a thousand bright-feathered birds alight on the miraculous tree, close by the Fountain of Life. Lunete weeps. The lion weeps. We all are filled with happiness.

"Yvain, you have emerged from your trials as a man," says Laudine, "and I believe that you love me. Stand by my side through all the joyous days to come. And when next thou visit Arthur's Court, I shall go with thee."

Come to rest, my proud-necked dun,
fold your paws, lion-hearted one,
twelve hundred leagues have all been run,
now foes are slain and honor's won,
now moon is swallowed by the sun,
now circle's closed and journey's done.

I am Yvain, the Knight of the Lion. This is my journey, and my story.

Author's Note

A whole treasury of legend celebrating the deeds of King Arthur and his knights was formed in Europe during the Middle Ages. These stories of adventure were drawn from the ancient epics of Ireland, Scotland, Wales, Cornwall, and Brittany. Bards—master storytellers—traveled from court to royal court entertaining with traditional tales. As they improvised for their audiences in song and poem, the bards gradually transformed the feats of ancient Celtic heros into the adventures of the Knights of the Round Table.

Poets and scholars, commissioned by aristocratic patrons, began to write down this rich material and the medieval romance emerged. These intricate and lengthy works were recited aloud to the enchantment of lords and ladies gathered before the bright hearths of great castles. The romance had become the most important literary form of the Middle Ages.

In *The Knight of the Lion*, the dark-haired youth Yvain sets out from Arthur's Court on a quest for glory. He aspires to perfect knighthood as demanded by the code of chivalry. Yvain rises, then swiftly falls, and must endure the ordeal of a second hero-journey more arduous than the first before he can attain true courage and compassion. I have based the outline of the story on the work of the twelfth-century French poet, Chrétien de Troyes. Chrétien was foremost among the many poets who wrote of the exploits of Arthur and his men. Around 1180, he composed *Yvain, ou Le Chevalier au Lion*, a verse romance of nearly seven thousand lines. Another version of the tale, apparently drawn from the same Celtic sources, was told by the Welsh bards and appears in the collection of romances called *The Mabinogian* as *The Lady of the Fountain*.

The choice of black and white art grew out of the dark power of the story itself. I have drawn the illustrations with calligraphic pen, India ink, and lithographic crayon on rough watercolor paper. The text type is 14 pt. Garamond Bold. The book was printed on 80 lb. Mohawk superfine white eggshell paper and is bound in cloth over boards. The binding is reinforced and Smyth sewn.

I would like to express my deep appreciation to my editor and publisher, Judith Whipple, for her guidance and unfailing support throughout a long and complex project. I am very grateful to Marianna Mayer, John Bierhorst, and John Tillinger for their critical comments and deep interest in my work. Special thanks to my designer, Jane Byers Bierhorst, for her aesthetic judgments and continual encouragement.

Background Reading

Chrétien de Troyes. *Arthurian Romances.* Translated by W. W. Comfort, New York: Dutton/Everyman's Library, 1975.

Huizinga, Johan. *The Waning of the Middle Ages.* London: E. Arnold and Co., 1924.

Jackson, W. T. H. *Medieval Literature: A History and a Guide.* New York: Macmillan, 1966.

Loomis, Roger Sherman. *Arthurian Tradition and Chrétien de Troyes.* New York: Columbia University Press, 1949.

Zimmer, Heinrich. *The King and the Corpse.* Edited by Joseph Campbell. Princeton: Princeton University Press, 1948.